LOOK WHAT I'VE GOT!

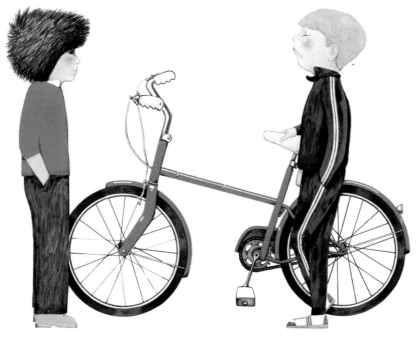

Anthony Browne

WALKER BOOKS

AND SUBSIDIARIES

LONDON · BOSTON · SYDNEY · AUCKLAND

First published 1980 by Julia McRae Books

This edition published 2010 by Walker Books Ltd
87 Vauxhall Walk, London SE11 5HJ

8 10 9 7

Printed in China

British Library Cataloguing in Publication Data:
a catalogue record for this book is available from the British Library

ISBN 978-1-4063-2625-3

www.walker.co.uk

For James
and Alex

Sam went for a walk.

Jeremy came by on his new bicycle.

"Look what I've got!" said Jeremy.
"I bet you wish you had one."

"Just watch me."

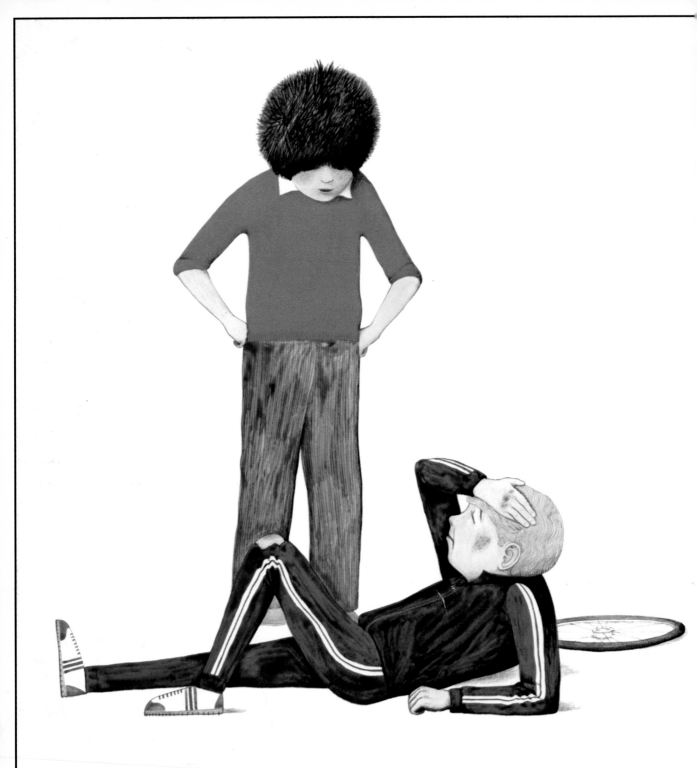

"Are you all right?" asked Sam.
Jeremy glared.

Sam went to the park.

Thud!

Jeremy was playing with his new football.
"Look what I've got!" he said. "I bet you
wish you had one."

They played football.

But Jeremy wasn't
very good.

Suddenly. . . .

Bang!

So Jeremy had
the ball . . .

. . . . Crash!

The park-keeper didn't seem very pleased.

Sam passed a shop. Jeremy came out
carrying an enormous bag of lollipops.

Look what I've got!" said Jeremy.
I bet you wish you had some."
He ate them all.

Jeremy sat down suddenly. . . .

Sam walked on, out of the town, towards the woods.

A gorilla leaped out at him.

am was terrified.

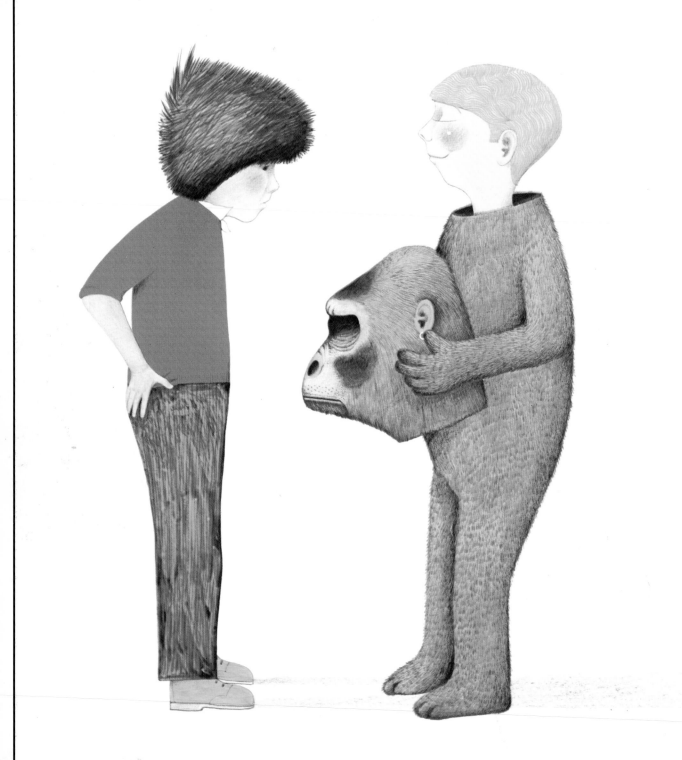

But it was Jeremy again.
"Look what I've got!" he said.
"I bet you wish you had one."

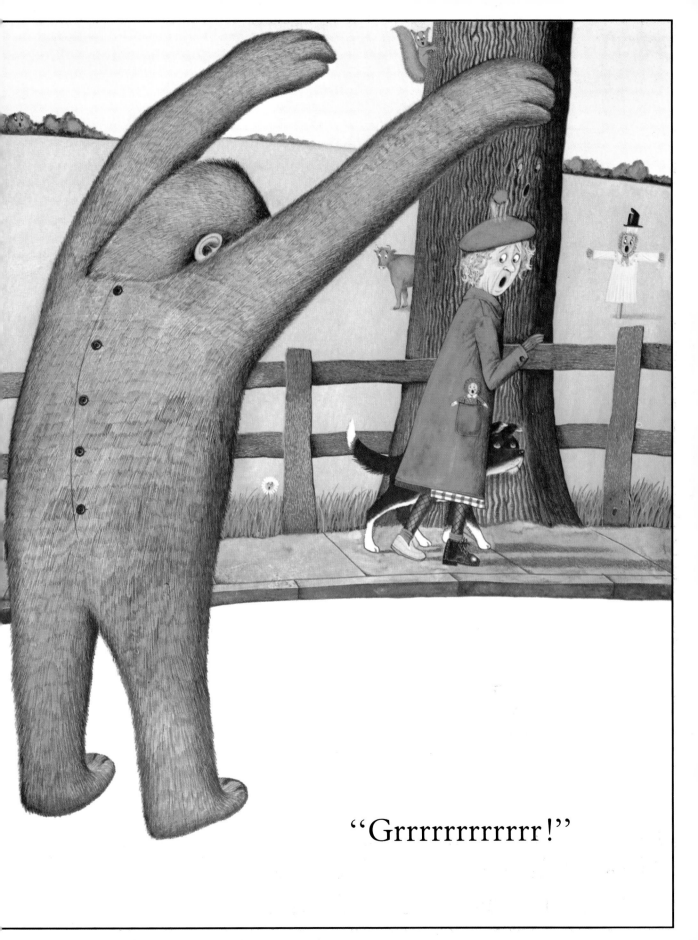

"Grrrrrrrrrr!"

But the old lady's dog was not frightened.

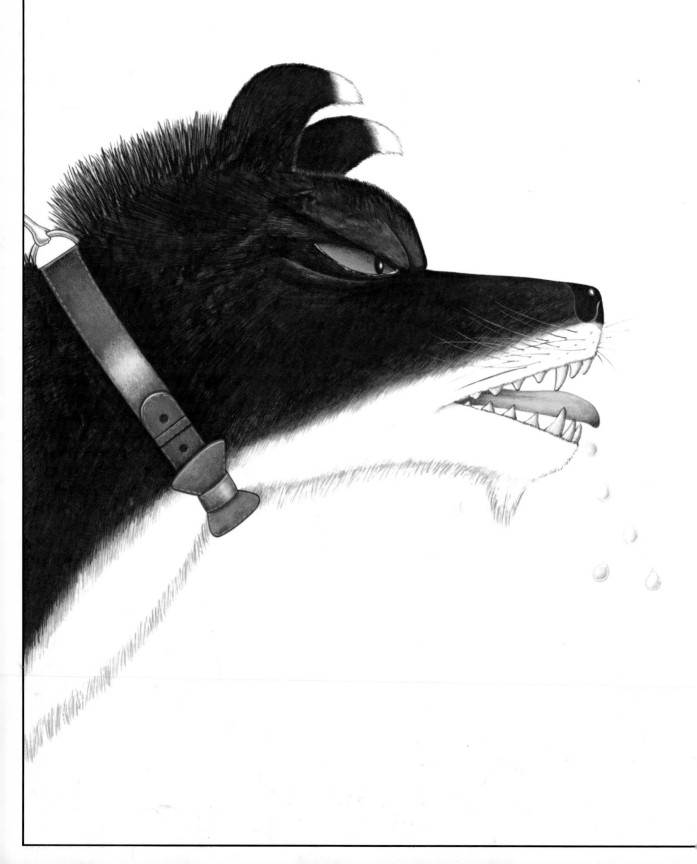

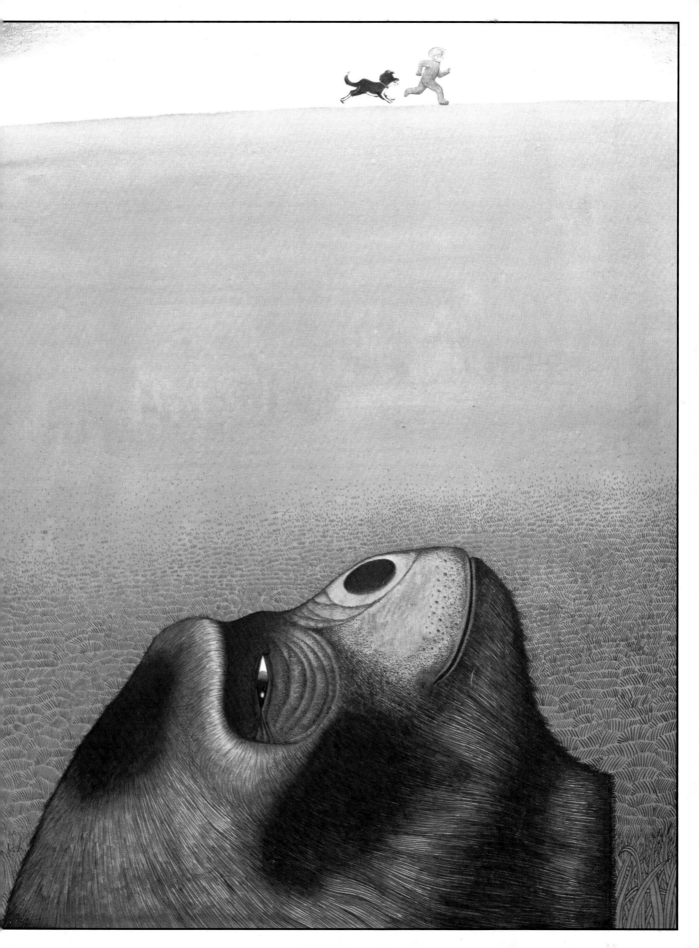

Sam stayed in the woods. Jeremy appeared.
"Look what I've got!" he said.
"I bet you wish you had one."

"No, not really," said Sam, and walked on.

But the wood was full of pirates.
They pounced on Jeremy.

The pirates made Jeremy walk the plank.

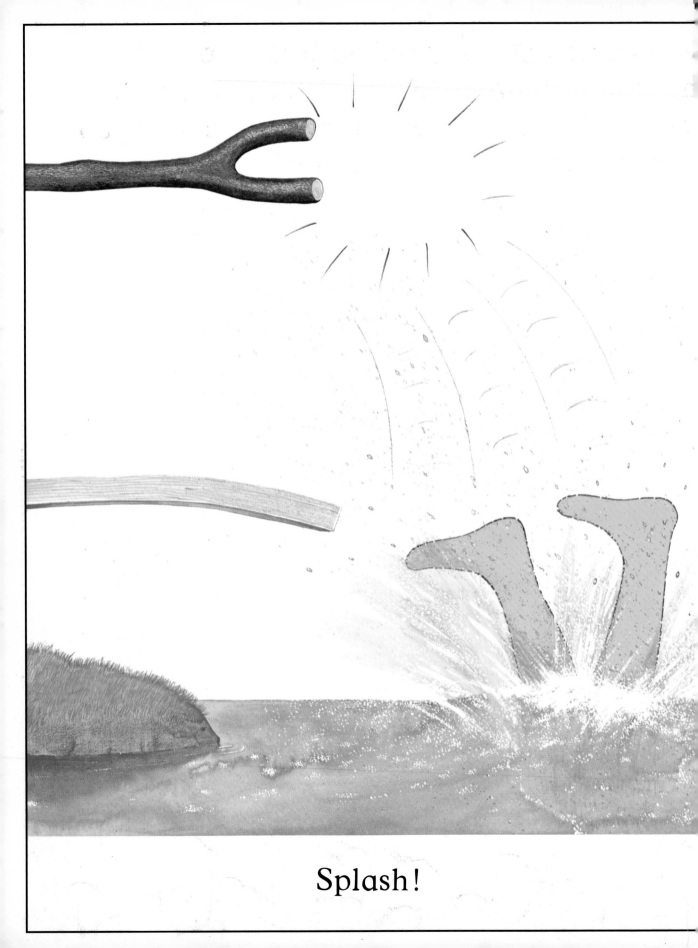

Splash!

am came back and pulled Jeremy out of
he water. "Hurry up," said Jeremy crossly.
My dad's taking me to the zoo this afternoon.
bet you wish you could come."

But Sam wasn't listening.